Jasmine's
SO Fussy

Published in paperback in 2016 by Wayland
Text © Wayland 2016
Illustrations © Jack Hughes 2016

Wayland
An imprint of Hachette Children's Group
Part of Hodder & Stoughton
Carmelite House, 50 Victoria Embankment
London EC4Y 0DZ

Commissioning Editor: Victoria Brooker
Design: Lisa Peacock and Alyssa Peacock

British Library Cataloguing in Publication Data
Heneghan, Judith.
Jasmine's SO fussy. -- (Dragon School)
1. Etiquette--Pictorial works--Juvenile fiction.
2. Children's stories--Pictorial works.
I. Title II. Series III. Hughes, Jack.
823.9'2-dc23

ISBN: 978 0 7502 8364 9

10 9 8 7 6 5 4 3 2 1

Printed in China

Wayland is a division of Hachette Children's Group,
an Hachette UK Company
www.hachette.co.uk

Jasmine's SO Fussy

Written by Judith Heneghan
Illustrated by Jack Hughes

WAYLAND

Jasmine was a happy dragon, most of the time. She knew what she liked, and she knew what she didn't like.

She liked to sit on her favourite log, for example.
But she didn't like sitting on the grass.

That didn't matter – did it?

One day, Brandon had some exciting news.
'There's going to be a party! Here, this afternoon!
We can help get everything ready!'
'Ooh!' said Noah. 'Let's have balloons and fancy
dress and strawberry cake!'

Jasmine frowned. She liked
parties, but she didn't
like strawberry cake.

First, the dragons decorated the clearing.
They had a bag of coloured balloons.
There were green ones and yellow ones
and red ones and blue ones.

Jasmine peered into the bag.
'Are there any purple ones?' she asked.
 'I don't think so,' said Brandon,
rummaging. 'What about yellow?'

'I don't like yellow,' said Jasmine.
'I only like purple.'

Next, Ruby made a list of party food.
'It's so hard to choose!' she said.
'I love rock burgers and fire cakes
and fruit drops and veggie bites and...'

Rock burgers

Fire cakes

Fruit drops

Veggie bites

'I don't like any of those things,'
said Jasmine. 'I only like jelly.'
Ruby stopped writing.
'You're being a bit fussy!' she told her.

Rock burgers

Fire cakes

uit

Veggie

This gave Brandon an idea.

'Let's pick berries in the forest,' he said.

'Then we can make some scrumptious berry jelly!'

But Jasmine trailed behind her friends as they walked beneath the trees. She didn't want berries in her jelly.

The forest was full of tasty strawberries and juicy blueberries and big green gooseberries.

'Wow!' exclaimed Noah. 'All this fruit looks amazing!'

'Aren't there any purple berries?' asked Jasmine.
'Try a strawberry instead,' suggested Brandon.
Jasmine shook her head. 'I won't like it,' she said.

When the food was ready,
Ruby pulled out the dressing up box.
'What shall I wear?' she wondered.
'This flower necklace or that pirate's hat?'

'I'm going to wear these fancy glasses,' said Noah.
'What are you going to wear, Jasmine?'

Jasmine looked in the box.
'I want to wear a cape,' she said,
'but there isn't one.'

'Well, here's a feathery scarf,' suggested Noah. 'You could wear that. But you probably don't like feathers.'

'No,' said Jasmine, sadly. 'I don't.'

The other dragons were beginning to feel cross.
'You're SO fussy!' said Brandon.
'Being fussy is BORING!' groaned Ruby.
'Why won't you try something DIFFERENT?' asked Noah.

Suddenly, Jasmine realised she wasn't looking forward to the party.

When the party started, the other dragons admired the costumes and balloons, as well as the plates of colourful food.

Jasmine didn't join in.

Jasmine's friends saw her sitting all alone.
She was being a bit silly, but they didn't
want her to feel left out.

So they hatched a plan.

'We've made something for you,' said Ruby.
'What is it?' asked Jasmine.
'A surprise,' said Brandon. 'You'll have
to close your eyes.'

'I don't like surprises...' wailed Jasmine.
'We think you'll like this one,' said Ruby.
Jasmine reluctantly closed her eyes.

Noah brought out the surprise.
Jasmine sniffed.
'That smells nice,' she said.

'Try some!' urged Brandon.

So Jasmine tried a tiny little bit.

'Mmm!' she said, licking her lips.

'It tastes yummy!' Then she opened her eyes.

'Oh!' she exclaimed.
'I didn't know I liked strawberry cake!'
'It's good to try new things,' said Noah.

'You're right,' said Jasmine. 'Being fussy IS silly.'
She grinned. 'From now on, I'm going to try
EVERYTHING! Let's go and have fun at the party!'